For Emilio, with love
from Dad and Ian

TRANSWORLD PUBLISHERS LTD
61-63 Uxbridge Road, London W5 5SA

TRANSWORLD PUBLISHERS c/o RANDOM HOUSE AUSTRALIA PTY LTD
20 Alfred Street, Milsons Point, NSW 2061

TRANSWORLD PUBLISHERS c/o RANDOM HOUSE NEW ZEALAND
18 Poland Road, Glenfield, Auckland

DOUBLEDAY CANADA LTD
105 Bond Street, Toronto, Ontario M5B IY3

Published 1999 by Doubleday
a division of Transworld Publishers Ltd

Text copyright © Ian Whybrow 1999
Illustrations copyright © Russell Ayto 1999
Designed by Ian Butterworth

The right of Ian Whybrow to be identified as the Author
and Russell Ayto as the illustrator of this work
has been asserted in accordance with
the Copyright, Designs and Patents Act 1988

A catalogue record for this book is available
from the British Library

ISBN 0 385 41023 9

0385 410 239 5126

Printed in Singapore
by Tien Wah Press

WHIFF

or HOW THE BEAUTIFUL BIG FAT SMELLY BABY FOUND A FRIEND

Ian Whybrow
Illustrated by Russell Ayto

DOUBLEDAY
London . New York . Toronto . Sydney . Auckland

By a bend in the river lived
a beautiful big fat smelly baby warthog.

His mum and dad were very proud of him.
They called him Whiff.
They wanted him to make friends and be happy.

The Crocodiles lived on one side.
The Monkeys lived on the other side.
And right across the street lived the Littlebirds.

But then... down came some tickly quickly flies!
They tickled their ears and they tickled their eyes.

So the crocodile bit his teddy bears,
He bashed the table and he crashed the chairs,
His teeth went snap and his tail went wheee!
Down fell the pictures, one-two-three!

So Whiff the beautiful big fat smelly
baby had to go home in disgrace.

So Whiff went next door to have tea with the Monkey babies.
He was on his best behaviour.

BUT... down came some tickly quickly flies! They tickled their ears and they tickled their eyes.

And cups and saucers flew through the air, And plates went flying everywhere!

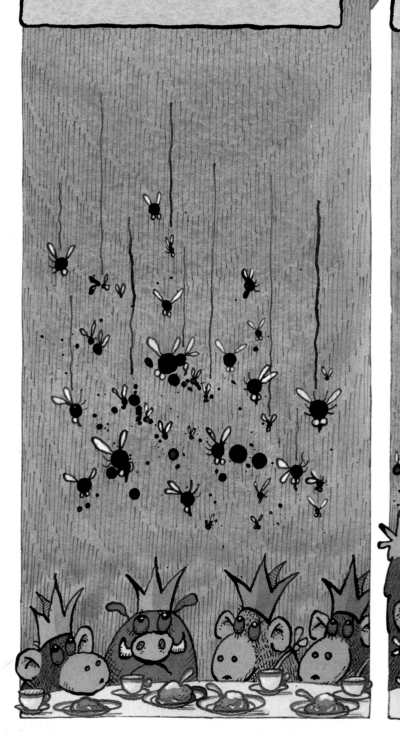

And the three
little monkeys were
jumping and squealing,
And jelly and custard
got stuck
on the ceiling!

So Whiff the beautiful big fat smelly baby had to go home in disgrace.

I think he is a good baby. But Mrs Crocodile says he is very rough. And Mrs Monkey says he is bad-mannered. They sent him home in disgrace.

And Mrs Littlebird said: "I can see he is beautiful. I can see he is big and fat. But tell me, is he *always* smelly?"

"Always," said Mrs Warthog.

"Never mind," said Mrs Littlebird. "Bring him over."

So Whiff went across the street
to play with Baby Littlebird.
They played happily for hours.
They played trains, planes, doctors and Jungle Monopoly.

But all of a sudden, with a

The baby bird
ate all the flies up!

And that is how the
beautiful big fat smelly baby
found a friend.